The Homeless Kitten

The Homeless Kitten

by Holly Webb
Illustrated by Sophy Williams

tiger tales

tiger tales

5 River Road, Suite 128, Wilton, CT 06897
Published in the United States 2018
Originally published in Great Britain 2007
by the Little Tiger Group
Text copyright © 2007 Holly Webb
Illustrations copyright © 2007 Sophy Williams
ISBN-13: 978-1-68010-423-3
ISBN-10: 1-68010-423-3
Printed in China
STP/1800/0192/0318
All rights reserved
10 9 8 7 6 5 4 3 2

For more insight and activities, visit us at www.tigertalesbooks.com

Contents

For everyone who has adopted a cat or kitten from a rescue—you are fabulous!

Chapter One
A Walk in the Woods

"You're coming with me, Lily? Are you sure?" Dad grinned at her, widening his eyes and pretending to be shocked.

"I like the sound of a walk with you and Hugo in the woods. It'll be nice and cool under the trees. Anyway—" Lily made a face back at him—"I'd come with you more often if you didn't go so fast. You both have really long legs, and

I don't." Lily reached down to rub the dog's soft creamy white ears. "Yes, you do, don't you? Great big long legs." She looked up at Dad. "You're not planning on one of your five-mile hikes, are you?" she asked suspiciously.

Dad laughed. "No, not in this weather—it's too hot for a long walk now. Anyway, I took Hugo out running with me early this morning."

Lily nodded. Hugo needed a lot of exercise. Dad took him for at least two long walks every day, and he usually went for a quick walk in the park with Mom when she stopped working to take a lunch break. On the weekend, Dad often took Hugo in the car to the hills just outside of town for a really good run. Lily's big sister, Carly, loved to go with them, but Lily wasn't a fan. It always seemed to rain when she went on one of Dad's big days out.

Hugo was mostly German shepherd —nobody was quite sure what else. Carly had told her that German shepherds were originally bred from dogs trained to guard flocks of sheep from wolves and bears. They were used to working hard. Dad had wanted a really energetic dog, and he'd fallen in love with Hugo at the animal rescue. He was so unusual with his white coat. The rescue staff said that Hugo had gotten too big for his elderly owner to take care of—and at the time, he hadn't even stopped growing.

Mom and Dad had explained to Lily and Carly that they'd have to be really gentle with him since he was a rescue dog, and because white German shepherds could be very sensitive and nervous. They were no good as pets for people who were out at work all day— if they were left alone, they could end up wrecking a house because they were so miserable! Luckily, Mom worked at home as a graphic designer, so Hugo was never by himself for long.

"Is Carly coming?" Dad asked. "Shout up the stairs for her, Lily."

"No, Mom's taking her over to Megan's house in a minute. Megan has one of those giant inflatable pools in her yard." Lily sighed enviously. It was the first week of summer vacation, and the weather was already so hot.

Even though it was sweltering, Hugo was still excited for his walk. He was standing by the front door staring at them both, his gleaming blue eyes hopeful. One of the boys in Carly's class had told her that Hugo was a spooky wolf dog because of his white coat and blue eyes, and Carly had gotten into trouble for chasing the boy around the playground. She adored Hugo even more than Dad did, and Hugo loved her to pieces.

Dad clipped on Hugo's leash and opened the front door. Hugo pulled Dad down the path, eager to be off, and Lily quickly slipped on her sneakers and hurried after them. "Bye, Mom! See you later, Carly!"

As they turned out of the gate, Hugo suddenly stiffened, his ears pricking forward and his tail flicking from side to side.

Dad peered over the fence, where Hugo was looking. "What are you so excited about? Oh! No, Hugo, no chasing cats."

"Is it Pixie?" Lily ran down the path to look. "Hello, sweetheart!" Pixie was a beautiful silvery tabby cat who belonged to their next-door neighbor,

Anna. Lily loved to play with Pixie—
so much that Carly was always teasing
her about it. Everyone else in the family
preferred dogs, but Lily's room was full
of cat posters and cat books…. Even
her pajamas had kittens on them.

Luckily for Lily, Pixie was always
popping into their yard. Sometimes she
even walked along the wall surrounding
the yard, and then hopped onto the
garage roof and in through Lily's
bedroom window. Lily loved to pretend
that Pixie was hers, but Mom always
shooed the cat out whenever she saw
her. She said it wasn't fair to Hugo,
letting a cat into his house.

Now the tabby cat was perched on
the fence, looking down disapprovingly
at Hugo, her tail swishing. Hugo had

never chased Pixie, but Lily thought he secretly wanted to. He didn't like her walking across his yard. He always stared at her out of the long windows in the living room, his nose pressed up against the glass. If Pixie hung around for too long, Hugo would let out a series of mighty barks.

Pixie rubbed her head against Lily's cheek, glared at Hugo, and jumped back down to the other side of the fence. Hugo barked and wagged his tail excitedly.

"Come on, boy," Dad said gently. "Walk time. Off to the woods."

Hugo shook himself and loped out onto the pavement, Dad and Lily jogging after him. The little wooded area they were going to wasn't far away—just a short walk up the hill.

"Ohhh, that's nice." Lily sighed happily, lifting her hair up off the back of her neck as they walked under the trees. "It's so much cooler here in the shade. Look, Hugo likes it, too. He must be so hot with all that thick fur."

Dad nodded. "I think this is one of Hugo's favorite places. So many good smells and all those squirrels."

"And sticks." Lily grinned. Hugo loved it when they threw sticks for him to chase after. "Are you going to let him off the leash?"

Dad looked around thoughtfully. Hugo was really good about coming back when he was called, but because he was so big, they had to be careful about letting him loose in case people were scared of him.

"I can't see anyone else…. Yes, we'll let him off for a minute. It's more fun for him sniffing around when he's off the leash."

As Hugo ambled ahead, Lily and Dad chatted about what they were going to do over the summer. They'd gone on a wonderful trip to a water park during Christmas vacation, so they weren't going away.

"I want to clean out the shed," Dad told Lily. "It's so full of junk, I can hardly get the lawnmower out."

"That's not very exciting!" Lily said, laughing. "You'll have to be careful though, Dad. Have you seen the size of the spiders in that shed? I went in there yesterday to get the water squirters, and I'm sure I saw one the size of my hand!"

"Yikes! I might wear gloves." Dad wrinkled his nose. "I suppose we should head back, since it's almost time for lunch. Hugo! Come on, boy!"

Hugo was a little ways away, gazing

curiously through the bushes, his tail wagging.

"Has he seen another dog?" Dad wondered, hurrying over. "Oh! Honestly. That's awful!"

"What is it?"

"Someone left a pile of stuff here instead of taking it to the dump." Dad pointed to a pile of furniture—an old couch and a fridge and what looked like some kitchen appliances. "What a mess! I'll have to call the sanitation department when we get home to see if they'll come and take it away. Someone must have driven down the alley to the garages at those houses—yes, look, the fence is broken. It wouldn't have been too hard to get the stuff through here."

"That's really sad." Lily looked at the mess, frowning. "Hey, Hugo. Where are you going, silly? That's not a couch for sitting on!" Hugo wasn't supposed to sit on any couches, but it was his one bad habit. He would lie at Dad's feet with his nose on the couch, and gradually creep further and further forward until he could sneak his front paws on. He never got very far before he was pushed off—but he never gave up trying, either. He just wanted to be snuggled up with his family.

"Here, boy, come on," Dad called. "Hugo!"

But Hugo didn't come back like he usually did. He was sniffing at the old couch, his fluffy tail swishing really fast.

"Maybe it smells like food," Dad

said, edging his way through the bushes to follow him. "It must smell like something. Look at him—he's really excited. Hugo, leave it, come on!"

Hugo's ears were pricked forward now, and he was whining and grunting and sniffing at the torn couch cushions.

Lily went after Dad, wriggling sideways through the undergrowth— she only had shorts on, and there were prickly leaves in among the bushes, but she wanted to see what Hugo was so excited about.

Hugo had his nose down the back of the couch cushions now. Then suddenly, he jumped back with a snort.

"What is it?" Lily asked, leaning over—and then she gasped.

Between the cushions and the back of the couch was a squirming mass of fur. A litter of tiny, fluffy kittens!

Chapter Two
A Surprising Discovery

"Kittens!" Lily gasped. "Oh, wow! Did Hugo smell them? Or maybe he heard something?"

The kittens were squirming around, making tiny squeaking noises. Hugo had moved the seat cushion with his nose while he was sniffing them out, so their cozy, dark nest had been disturbed. Now the big dog was staring down at the kittens with his ears pricked forward again. Dad had put a hand on his collar, just in case. After all, Hugo really didn't like Pixie, so it made sense that he wouldn't like the kittens, either. But right now he looked interested rather than grumpy.

Lily crouched down next to Hugo so she could look, too. There were three kittens—two tabbies and a beautiful, little white kitten. Their fur looked very long and fluffy to Lily, longer than Pixie's, she was sure. Maybe they were going to be longhairs, like Persians. But they didn't have squashed Persian noses.

"I don't understand." Lily looked around. "Why would anyone put kittens down the back of a couch? They should have taken them to an animal rescue, not just dumped them in the woods. What a horrible thing to do!"

Dad nodded. "It is weird. Unless.... Yes, that could be it. Maybe it was the mother cat."

"You mean, she had her babies out here in the woods?" Lily looked doubtful. "Why would a cat want to have kittens in a grubby old couch?"

"Cats do pick funny places sometimes. I remember Grandma telling me that her cat had a litter of kittens in her wardrobe when she was a little girl."

"But why the woods instead of at home?" Lily looked up at Dad anxiously.

"Maybe the mom doesn't have a home," Dad replied.

Lily thought for a moment. "Do you think she might be a stray?"

"Could be," Dad agreed. He glanced around, peering through the trees. "I wonder where she is. They look too small to be left alone for very long."

Just then the white kitten wriggled around and let out a squeaky little meow. Lily laughed delightedly. He— or she—was so cute, with a tiny pink nose and blue eyes. Even though his eyes were open, Lily didn't think he could really see her—his eyes didn't seem to be focusing. He was weaving his head around, though, sniffing at the air. Lily wondered if he could smell Hugo. Or maybe he was just upset that their mom had left and their nest had been disturbed.

"If their eyes are open, that means they have to be a few days old, doesn't it?" Lily said, trying to think. She'd read somewhere that kittens were born with their eyes closed.

"Yes." Dad nodded. "I think so. But I'm still pretty sure they need their mom. They're too young to be walking around—they're just squirming around and wriggling on top of each other, aren't they?" He looked around again. "There's no sign of the mother cat. I wonder what's best to do."

"Don't you think we should take them home, Dad?" Lily said pleadingly. "We can't leave them out here on their own, not when they're so little. They can't find any food for themselves, can they? Don't they still need their mom's milk?"

Dad shook his head. "Their mom could just have gone looking for food—she might be back any minute. Or maybe she actually is around here somewhere but she's too scared of us to come back to her kittens. I mean, no cat's going to walk up to Hugo...."

Hugo was still watching the kittens as though they were the best thing he'd ever seen. He was following them with his nose as they clambered over and around each other, still squeaking.

"I think he likes them," Lily said, smiling. But then her smile faded. "What are we going to do, Dad? We can't just leave them and hope their mom comes back. What if she doesn't? They need her. Or somebody to take care of them, anyway."

Dad frowned. "You know what? I'm going to call the animal rescue where we got Hugo. I've got their number in my phone. I bet they'll know what to do."

Lily nodded. That was definitely a good idea. The staff at the rescue must have to deal with abandoned kittens all the time. She listened as her dad called and explained about the kittens.

"No, we haven't seen the mom at all. Do you think she won't come back while we're here? No, I suppose not, if she's a stray…. So, what do you think? Should we leave them?"

"Oh, no…," Lily whispered to herself, looking over at the tiny kittens. The little white one had ended up underneath the other two now. Lily longed to pick him up—surely it couldn't be good for him to be squished like that….

She breathed a sigh of relief as he wriggled out and accidentally nudged

Hugo's nose with his own. Hugo stepped back, surprised, and Lily giggled.

"You like them, don't you?" Lily whispered to Hugo as he rested his chin on the arm of the couch, gazing at the kittens.

Lily turned back to Dad. The rescue couldn't be telling him to leave the kittens here! She couldn't bear to think of them all on their own.

"I'm really not sure how long she's been away, that's the thing," her dad was saying. "Woodland Trails. That's right. Yes, we could do that. Will there be someone answering the phone later this evening? Okay, I'll get back to you then. Thanks."

"What did they say?" Lily burst out.

"They think the mom's probably right here somewhere, hiding out and watching until we leave."

"Oh…." Lily looked around the woods, golden and silent in the sunlight. "But what if she's not? What if she doesn't come back?"

"Well, that's the problem. If she doesn't, I'm afraid the kittens won't last long without her. They're just too little to survive by themselves. They'll have to be taken to the rescue for hand-rearing—that means someone feeding them with a special bottle. So, we need to see what happens."

Dad made an apologetic face at Lily. "I said we'd keep an eye on them and watch out for their mom, Lils. It might be a little boring. The lady from the rescue said we needed to give the mother cat a few hours before we do anything like moving the kittens."

"I don't mind! I don't want to leave them—even Hugo doesn't. Look at him!"

Dad nodded. "He's really fascinated,

isn't he? It's funny when you think how he is about Pixie. Maybe he doesn't understand that these are cats, too...." He smiled at Lily. "I'm sure the mom will appear if we get out of her way. Come on, Hugo." He looked around the clearing as Hugo paced over to his side. "We need to find somewhere to watch from."

Lily stepped back reluctantly from the couch and the kittens. The white kitten was on the top of the pile now, weaving his head from side to side. She longed to pick him up and cuddle him, and tell him everything was going to be okay, but she knew she shouldn't....

The white kitten meowed, calling miserably for his mother. He wanted milk—he kept stumbling around, trying to suck, but his mom wasn't there. He didn't understand. She had always been there to feed him before. She seemed to have been gone for so long, and he was so hungry.

He hooked his tiny claws into the fabric at the back of the couch and hauled himself up, sniffing the air, trying to find his mother. There was no warm, milky smell, but he could smell something else, something different. He meowed uncertainly and sniffed the air again. The smell seemed to have moved away. Confused and worn out by the effort, he nuzzled into the furry pile of other kittens and settled back to sleep.

Chapter Three
Keeping Watch

"Lily, are you sure you don't want to go home?" Dad asked. "Mom just texted. She says she can walk up and get you and take Hugo back, too. We've been watching for an hour now. You must be getting hungry—it's past lunchtime."

Lily shook her head firmly. "I don't want to go home. And I don't mind not having any lunch."

They were sitting on a fallen tree with Hugo at their feet, just close enough to see the abandoned couch through the bushes. Lily was pretty sure they were far enough away not to worry the mother cat, as long as they were quiet. The couch wasn't that far from the main paths through the woods, so she must have been coming and going with

people and dogs around.

"Please, Dad," Lily begged as Dad started to text Mom back. "I really want to stay and make sure the kittens are okay. I know we've been here an hour, but that's an hour that their mom hasn't come back to take care of them. That can't be right, can it? She's been gone a long time."

Dad nodded. "It does seem like a long time to me, but I'm not really sure how often tiny kittens need to be fed. I don't think we can stay here all day, Lily. Maybe we can keep popping back to check on them."

"But there are so many people who walk their dogs in these woods," Lily pointed out. "I know Hugo just wants to look at the kittens, but another dog might hurt them."

They'd seen quite a few dog walkers already, but luckily none of the dogs had come close enough to sniff out the kittens. Dad had asked the owners if they'd seen a cat around, but they'd all said no. One lady had even offered to go home and call the animal rescue when Dad and Lily told her about the kittens but Dad had explained that they'd already called the rescue.

"Okay," Dad said, putting his phone away. "I told Mom we'll stay."

"What do you think could have happened to their mom?" Lily asked a little while later. "I don't think she's coming back, Dad. Why would she leave them?"

Dad sighed. "I don't know. Maybe she just couldn't take care of them. The lady from the rescue did say when very young cats have kittens, they do sometimes abandon them. Because they just don't have the energy to feed themselves and make enough milk for the kittens, too. If she's a stray and she's having to hunt for her food, or steal it out of garbage cans, she might not be able to cope."

"That's so sad." Lily sighed, thinking of Pixie next door—so plump and well fed.

"Or it could be that she's not a stray. Maybe she just came here to have her kittens, and now her family has found her and they're keeping her in to keep her from going off again."

"But they must know the kittens need her!" Lily shook her head. "Nobody would be that mean!"

Dad nodded. "No, you're probably right. I'm sure the owners would want to take care of the kittens. Unless maybe they didn't realize she was pregnant…?"

Dad looked over toward the gap in the fence and the alley that led down to the houses and frowned. "Lily, listen, love. I don't want to upset you, but there is another thing that could have happened. It's a busy road out there. The mother could have been hit by a car."

Lily swallowed, and her voice wobbled when she answered. "I know. I was thinking about that. We go down that road to school, and cars do go really fast along there. Do you think she tried to cross it?"

"If she doesn't come back, we'll probably never know." Dad put his arms around her shoulders. "But it's a possibility."

41

"Poor cat," Lily whispered. "And poor kittens."

"Well, at least we found them, thanks to Hugo."

"He's a hero." Lily rubbed his nose, and Hugo turned to look back at her for a moment. Then his ears twitched and he stood up, gazing down the path. "Someone's coming," Lily said. "Oh, it's Mom! And Carly! But I said I didn't want to go back, Dad."

"Hello!" Lily's mom stood on tiptoe, trying to see the couch and the kittens. "We thought we'd come and bring you some sandwiches. Are they over there?"

"Can I go and see?" Carly asked.

"Just quickly," Dad suggested. "We're watching for their mom, Carly. We don't want to scare her off."

As Mom and Carly hurried over to take a quick look, Hugo stood up, whining a little.

"It's okay, boy." Dad patted him reassuringly. "He really is keeping watch over those kittens, isn't he?"

"They're beautiful," Mom whispered as she and Carly came creeping back through the bushes. "But so tiny! Surely they're going to need feeding soon?"

Dad nodded. "I think so. But the

lady at the rescue told us not to do anything until this evening. Just watch and wait."

"Lily, you're sure you don't want to come home with us? You've been out here for such a long time."

Lily shook her head. "Not yet, Mom, please. I'm so worried about them—and their mom," she added sadly. "Dad thinks she might have been run over."

"Oh, Lily." Mom hugged her.

"It's so lucky that Hugo sniffed them out," Lily said.

"I was going to say that we'd take him back," Mom said thoughtfully. "But looking at him, I'm not sure he'd come. He's had his eyes fixed on that couch the entire time since we arrived. Maybe he thinks that because he found the kittens, he has to keep an eye on them." She was smiling, but she sounded half-serious.

Lily nodded. "German shepherds are often guard dogs, aren't they? Hugo is guarding the kittens."

Chapter Four
An Unexpected Problem

Lily leaned forward eagerly, certain she'd seen a flash of white close by the old couch. Maybe the kittens' mom was a white cat—that would make sense. She started to say, "Dad…," but then she sighed. It wasn't the cat after all. Just an old plastic bag, flapping in the breeze.

She shivered a little. Even though

it had been such a hot day, the woods were shady, especially now that the sun was starting to go down. She peered over at the couch, wondering if the kittens were feeling chilly, too. She and Dad had gone to check on them after Mom and Carly had left, and pulled the cushion back over them a little, but she couldn't help worrying.

Over in the clearing, the white kitten huddled closer to his sisters, hunting for some warmth. Usually they were all snuggled up together against their mother, but without her body heat, the kittens were so small that they couldn't keep themselves warm. He was getting colder and colder, and it was getting hard to move. He squeaked for his mother again, calling to her to come back and feed them, but she didn't come. Exhausted and hungry, the tiny kitten tried to crawl further under the cushions.

Lily shifted position again. She was getting pins and needles from sitting still for so long, and she was hungry. The sandwiches Mom had brought felt like a long time ago. She checked her watch. "Dad, it's six o'clock," she said, stretching out her feet and wriggling a bit.

"I know. I'm going to call the rescue. It's been seven hours now." He took out his phone, and Lily leaned closer to try to listen in.

48

"Hi, I called earlier about some kittens our dog had found in Woodland Trails. No, no sign of their mom coming back, I'm afraid. Would you be able to come and get them?"

He paused for a minute or so, listening, and Lily saw an anxious expression appear on his face—little creases over the top of his nose. "Oh…. No, don't do that. Maybe we can help. Let me talk to my wife and get back to you." He listened for a little longer, saying, "Mm-hm, mm-hm," and Lily squeezed even closer, desperate to know what was going on.

"Dad, what happened?" she burst out as soon as he ended the call.

"The rescue is really full. All of their foster families have kittens already.

49

The manager was saying that she'd call around and see who could squeeze them in. Apparently, this is kitten season." He laughed a little nervously.

"So what's going to happen to our kittens?" Lily asked. "Will they go to one of these foster people? Will they be all right?"

Dad was silent for a minute, running his hand down the back of Hugo's neck. "Actually, Lily, I'm wondering if we could take them. Just until they find someone else."

"What?" Lily squeaked. She was so surprised and excited that she actually jumped up and down. "Do you mean it? We can take them home?"

"Hold on! Slow down a minute. I'm only talking about us taking care of them until there's space for them with a foster family. Since it's an emergency. And I said I'd have to talk to your mom about it. There's no point getting excited just yet."

"I know." Lily's voice was shaking. Those tiny kittens, hers to take care of! If only Mom would say yes! She watched eagerly as Dad called home.

"Sarah, it's me. Yes, I called them, but there's a problem—apparently they're really full. The lady I spoke to earlier didn't realize it, but all their kitten foster families already have litters of kittens. No, we're not going to leave them! What do you think about us taking care of them for a little while? The rescue manager, the one I just spoke to, said she'd send someone out to help us take them home. They'll bring some kitten formula and some information on how to care for them if we agree."

He went quiet for a minute, and Lily pressed closer. She could hear her mom's voice in the background, and she wished Dad had put the speaker on.

"Yes, I know. The rescue manager mentioned that. I can't say I'm happy about getting up in the middle of the night, but I feel responsible for them. They're so little—"

"Dad, what's the matter?" Lily interrupted. "What's Mom saying? Why can't we do it?"

"Because they're so young, they'll need hand-rearing, Lily. Mom isn't sure we'll be up to it—we'd probably have to get up in the middle of the night."

Lily grabbed his arm. "But I could help! Couldn't I? It's summer vacation, and I don't mind. Dad, please! It's like we were meant to find them—we came along just at the right time. We can't give up on them now!"

Dad sighed. "Did you hear all that?" he said into the phone. "Yes, I know. Maybe she is old enough to help out.

You know how much she loves cats!"

"Okay." Dad smiled at Lily. "Yes, I'll call the rescue back and tell them." He ended the call and laughed. "Wow. This was definitely not what I was expecting when we came out for a walk this morning."

"We'll put them in here," Amy explained, showing Lily and Dad a cardboard travel box that she'd brought with her. Lily thought that she seemed really nice. She'd told them she remembered Hugo from the rescue and that he'd grown into such a handsome, well-behaved dog.

"I've put a hot-water bottle in for them, wrapped up in some towels. If they've been without their mom all day, they'll be getting really cold. Kittens this young can't control their own temperature. They need their mom's body heat to keep them warm. Even though it's been so hot today, if we  leave them here overnight without her, they're at risk of hypothermia—that's getting too cold to survive."

"How old do you think they are?" Lily asked, leaning over to look at the kittens. They were still moving— squirming around and nuzzling at each other—but she was sure they weren't as lively as they had been when she first saw them.

"Hard to say, exactly. Maybe two to three weeks? Their eyes are open, but they don't look big enough to be walking yet. Soon, though."

"They don't look as bright as they did this morning," Dad said.

"I was thinking that, too." Lily bit her lip. "Oh, no. Maybe we waited too long to see if their mom would come back."

Amy shook her head. "I don't think so. I know it sounds hard, but the best one to take care of them is definitely their mom—she's built for feeding them, cleaning them, and keeping them warm. If we take them away from her, we're giving the kittens second-best. Do you see what I mean? So if there'd been any chance that their mom was going to come back and care for them, it was better to let her."

"Dad thinks she might have been run over," Lily said, gazing down at the kittens.

Amy nodded. "It's possible, I'm afraid. Or she may just not have been able to feed them. Either way, I think we have to assume she's not coming back."

She opened the travel box, then gently reached down to pick up one of the tabby kittens. Hugo whined and Amy laughed. "You're such a good boy, aren't you? Are you taking over for their mom, Hugo?"

She put the kitten gently into the box, and Hugo nosed at the cardboard flaps, clearly making sure that the kitten was all right. "We wouldn't usually put foster kittens with a family who has a dog, but this is a bit of an emergency. Now, I'll come back to the house with you, if that's okay, and help you set up a safe area to keep them in."

Amy picked up the other tabby kitten, and Lily watched anxiously as the white kitten gave a feeble meow. The kitten looked so little, left all on his own. "Can I pick this one up?" Lily whispered. He was hardly moving.

"Sure."

Lily picked up the tiny kitten—he wasn't much bigger than her cupped hands—and carefully moved him over to the box. He squirmed around and gave another squeaky breath of a meow, but then he cuddled

59

up next to the two tabby kittens again, snuggling against the warmth of the hot-water bottle.

Lily looked up at Dad with shining eyes. "Let's take them home."

Chapter Five
Settling In

Amy came back to the house to help
settle the kittens in. She brought in a
big box of equipment from her car—
special kitten milk and kitten bottles
and a litter box. She explained that the
kittens would need feeding about every
four hours. "It's a lot of work," she said,
looking around at them all. "Are you
really sure you can manage?"

Mom was reading the instruction sheets, looking rather anxious. "Oh my goodness, I hadn't even thought about sterilizing," she said. "But I suppose it's just like feeding a baby. Do we still have the old sterilizer in the attic?"

Dad grinned. "Yes. Now aren't you glad that I never sorted all that stuff out to donate to charity? I'll go and get it. We need to give them a feeding as soon as possible, don't we?"

"Yes, that would be great." Amy looked happy. "Having a sterilizer will definitely make things easier. Oh!" Amy turned around from the table. Hugo had nudged open the kitchen door and marched in, looking determined.

"I'm sorry—I'll take him out again." Mom shook her head. "No, Hugo. You need to stay away from the kittens. It's going to be tricky keeping him out, since he's used to having his basket and food bowls in here."

"Wait a minute," Dad said. "Look at him. He's not bothered at all that they're in his kitchen. Even though we've moved his basket away from the radiator and put the box there instead."

Amy nodded. "I think you're right. And I was going to say that I'd try and get hold of a special heating pad for you, to keep the kittens warm, but I'm not sure you're going to need it."

The kittens were still in their cardboard box, curled up on the hot-water bottle, but now Hugo lay down and curled himself around it so that they had his warmth, too. The kittens were already pressing up against the side of the box next to him. Even though they were so tiny, their instincts were telling them to warm up.

"Hugo really loves them." Lily smiled. She'd never have expected that Hugo would make such a wonderful kitten nurse.

"He sure does," Amy smiled. Then she continued, "I'll show you how to mix the milk powder and feed the kittens. And then—well, for another week or so, until they're old enough to do it themselves, I'm afraid you're going to have to help them pee and poop afterward."

"That's disgusting!" Carly said, making a horrified face.

Amy laughed. "I know it sounds weird. But mother cats lick their kittens after they've fed them, and that tells their bodies to pee or poop. When you're hand-rearing kittens, you have to do everything their mom does, but with a cotton ball, dampened with warm boiled water," she added hurriedly.

"Thank goodness for that," Dad replied.

The white kitten woke up and looked around the dark room. He still couldn't see or smell his mother, but at least he was warm. He remembered being fed, too, but now he was feeling hungry again. He staggered up onto his paws and meowed, calling for his mother. But instead of a fluffy tabby face, a large white nose came over the side of his box and nuzzled at him.

The kitten sniffed and then sneezed and looked up at the huge creature in confusion. This was most definitely not his mother. Whoever it was felt warm, though, and comforting. The kitten meowed again, asking the big dog for food, and felt his two tabby sisters stirring beside him. They started to call for milk, too.

The kitten moved his head toward the sounds and then let out a tiny squeak of his own. Hugo had leaned down again and picked him up—just the way his mother did—in his jaws. The kitten wriggled as he was lifted from the box, but then he found himself between the dog's big paws, cozily nestled against the thick fur of his chest. Forgetting to be hungry for a moment, the kitten snuggled closer and drifted back to sleep.

Upstairs, Lily lay half awake. She'd been dreaming about the kittens, and now she couldn't tell whether she was asleep or not. She could hear meowing—pitiful little squeaks—and low voices coming from downstairs. Of course! The nighttime feeding!

Mom and Dad had figured out that it would be best to feed the kittens at about eleven o'clock before they went to bed, then at three in the morning, and then again when they all got up. Dad had said it would only be for a week or so, until the kittens were a little older and could go for more than four hours without food.

Lily had begged to be allowed to help, but Mom and Dad had said it was much too late for her and Carly, even though it was summer vacation.

But if they were feeding the kittens, why could she hear meowing? The little squeaks sounded desperate. Lily sat up worriedly. She had to make sure they were okay—especially the fluffy white one. He had felt so tiny in her hands when she lifted him into the box, as though there was hardly anything under all that fur.

Lily got out of bed, pulled on her robe, and fumbled sleepily for her slippers. Then she crept down the stairs.

69

She tiptoed along the hallway and peered into the kitchen. Her mom and dad were sitting at the table in their pajamas, each with a tabby kitten in their laps. The kittens were busily sucking from the bottles.

"Lily! You should be asleep!" Dad sighed.

"I could hear meowing, and it woke me up. What's wrong?"

"It's a little tricky feeding more than one at once—the white kitten was asleep, so we thought we'd leave him until last, but now he's woken up and he's not happy about waiting," Mom explained. "I'm sure he can smell the milk."

Lily was just about to crouch down and peer into the box when Hugo gave a mournful "Arrrooo!" and she realized that he had the kitten between his paws.

"Oh, Hugo's taking care of him!"

"He lifted the kitten out of the box in his mouth," Dad told her. "I was a little worried. But then I think mother cats do the same thing."

"Is all that meowing bothering you, Hugo?" Lily asked. Then she turned back to look at Mom and Dad. "Can I feed him? Since I'm awake anyway? We have another bottle, and Hugo's getting upset. He doesn't like Stanley crying like that."

"Stanley?" Mom smiled at her. "Since when is he named Stanley?"

Lily turned pink. "I just think he looks like a Stanley. It's such a cute name."

"It is cute," Mom agreed, passing Lily a bottle. "But just remember we're not going to have them for long, Lily. Only until the rescue can find a foster home."

"I know." Lily gently scooped up the white kitten and carried him over to the table. Hugo followed her, resting his muzzle on her lap so he could watch what she was doing. Stanley seemed to have learned exactly what to do with the bottle from his two previous feedings—he practically jumped at it, sucking greedily at the milk with funny little slurping noises.

"Wow, you really were hungry," Lily said. "Mom, look! I think I can actually see his tummy getting bigger!"

Her mom laughed. "They're really guzzling it down, aren't they? Oh, Lily, listen!"

"I can feel it…," Lily whispered back. Stanley was purring.

Chapter Six
Kitten Playtime

"Which one's your favorite?" Nora leaned over the kittens' box, admiring the three kittens. Lily had emailed her best friend to tell her about their amazing discovery, and Nora had been desperate to come and see the kittens as soon as she'd gotten back from her vacation in Mexico.

They were about five weeks old

now—big enough to walk around really well. They stomped all over each other, squeaking loudly, and they were always wrestling and jumping at each other. They loved playing with all the toys Lily had persuaded Mom and Dad to get from the pet store, too. Their favorite was a feathery stick, a little like a feather duster, and Lily spent a lot of time waving it around for them.

Dad had found a big, shallow plastic storage box up in the attic when he was looking for the sterilizer, and he'd brought it down to use as a pen to keep the kittens in. It meant they had space to move around, but they were safer than they would be loose in the kitchen. But it hadn't lasted long. They still used it to sleep in, but they'd learned to wriggle

75

and scramble their way out after just a few days.

"Stanley—he's my favorite," Lily said, pointing him out. "He's like a little fluffy snowball!"

"He is cute," Nora agreed. "But I love the stripes on the other two as well. Isn't it a lot of work taking care of them all?"

"They're starting to eat solid food now—special kitten food mixed with a little bit of their milk. At least that means we can just feed them really late at night and then early in the morning. No one has to get up in the middle of the night anymore." Lily reached her hand into the plastic box, and Stanley staggered determinedly toward her, licking at her fingers.

"They're so beautiful. If it were me,

I don't think I'd be able to give them away," Nora said, lifting one of the tabby kittens onto her lap. They were both girls, and Carly had named them Bella and Trixie. "You've spent your entire summer vacation taking care of them, but then you don't get to keep them. That doesn't seem fair!"

"I know." Lily sighed. "But we were never going to keep them. They were originally supposed to go to another foster family as soon as they had the space. But when Amy came to check up on them a couple of days after they came here, she said we were doing so well that maybe we should just keep them until they were ready for adoption. And luckily Mom and Dad said yes!" She smiled as Stanley butted his head against her hand and let out a squeaky little meow. "It's not food time yet, baby...."

"So they won't go to the rescue, then?"

"Their photos are up on the rescue website already, but they'll just send anyone who's interested in adopting them over to us. So at least the kittens won't have to get used to a new place."

Nora nodded. "And you'll be able to see if the people are nice."

Lily nodded. She didn't like thinking about the kittens' new owners—especially not Stanley's. Even though she was making the best of it to Nora, she couldn't imagine not having a box of kittens in their kitchen.... But they already had Hugo.

"Do you think Hugo will miss them?" Nora asked as she heard scratching at the kitchen door.

Lily opened the door, checking that the kittens weren't about to dart through, and Hugo trotted in, immediately coming over to inspect his kittens.

"Definitely." Lily petted his nose. "He

does that every time he's been out for a walk. He has to come back and make sure they're all okay. Yes, don't worry—I took care of them for you. Trixie's over there, see?"

Hugo was looking around for the other tabby kitten, and when he spotted her peeking out from behind the garbage can, he went to round her up, gently nosing her back over toward the plastic box.

"He wants them all in the box the entire time," Lily explained. "He's like a sheepdog, herding them together." She watched proudly as Hugo picked up the tabby kitten in his mouth and dropped her, wriggling, back into the box.

"I thought he was biting her!" Nora said, looking a bit worried.

"No. He's so gentle. He just holds them in his mouth. Their mom would have done the same thing. Oh, Hugo, look—Stanley's coming out now."

The white kitten was clambering out of the box, half falling, half jumping out onto the kitchen tiles. Hugo seemed almost to sigh. He lay down in front of the box between the two girls, making a big furry barrier between Stanley and the rest of the kitchen.

Stanley nuzzled him, nose to nose, and both girls "aaahhed." Stanley marched along the length of Hugo and started to pat at his feathery tail as Hugo twitched it from side to side, and then jumped on it with fierce little growls. Hugo watched him, clearly enjoying the game. As soon as Stanley was clinging on with all four paws, he swished his tail faster so that the kitten swept across the floor, and both girls burst out laughing.

"They get along so well," Nora said. "They're both white and fluffy."

"I know." Lily nodded. They really did. If only they could keep Stanley, he and Hugo would be a perfect pair.

Lily giggled as Stanley wobbled down her bed. He wasn't very good at walking on the squishy comforter, and he kept almost falling over. He stopped to inspect her teddy bear and then jumped at it, sinking his tiny claws into the ribbon around its neck.

Lily was so busy watching Stanley that she didn't notice the gentle scuffling noises from outside her bedroom window. Then there was a loud hiss, and she glanced around in surprise. Pixie was standing on the sloping roof, peering in at the open window, the fur on the back of her neck raised. She was clearly furious—this was the place she liked to visit, and now there was another cat.

"Oh, Pixie, no!" Lily stared at her anxiously. What was she going to think of Stanley? She'd been in Lily's room a couple of times since they'd gotten the kittens, but Lily had quickly shut her door so that Pixie didn't go downstairs. This was the first time Pixie had seen one of them.

Lily hesitated, not sure whether to grab Stanley or try to shoo Pixie out. She didn't want to push her back through the window in case she slipped. Pixie came further in, climbing onto Lily's windowsill and hissing loudly, her tail fluffing up.

"No!" Lily said sharply, seeing Stanley cower back against the teddy bear, his own fur starting to stand up, too. "Pixie, out! This isn't your house!"

She sat up, trying to grab Pixie. Maybe she could take her downstairs and put her out the front door. "I know you've been in here before, but I'm sorry, Pixie. Ow!" Pixie had swiped her paw down Lily's arm, leaving two bright red scratches. Then she hissed again, spat angrily at Stanley, and darted back out the window.

Lily shut the window, rather shakily. Pixie had never scratched her before. Then she glanced at Stanley. He was huddled into a tiny white ball on her bed, and he looked terrified.

"Oh, Stanley, I'm sorry, sweetheart. It's okay. She's not coming back in." Gently, Lily lifted him up in her cupped hands and snuggled him against her T-shirt.

"It's all right. I'll take care of you. I wish I could just take care of you always," she added sadly. The rescue had called Mom that morning to say a lady had seen the kittens on their website and wanted to come and visit them. She was interested in the two tabbies, but Lily knew it wouldn't

86

be long before someone wanted to take Stanley, too.

Stanley huddled against her, his heart thumping. He didn't understand what had just happened. He had been happy playing with Lily by himself, without his sisters climbing all over her, too. He loved it when she gave him attention and played with him and then let him sleep on her lap when he was tired out. But suddenly the other cat had appeared, one that Stanley had never seen before.

Hugo nosed his way around Lily's door and padded across the room.

"Did you hear Pixie?" Lily asked him. "She was really angry. Oh, you can smell her, can't you?"

Hugo's ears had flattened back, and he was sniffing at Lily's bed. Then he nudged Stanley gently. The white kitten rubbed his head against the huge dog's muzzle and then stepped back with a squeak as Hugo licked him, his big pink tongue practically covering the tiny kitten.

"Hugo!" Lily giggled. "Look at him! You've flattened his fur!"

"They're so beautiful…. I wish we could take all of them, but I think three cats might be too many." Candace smiled at Lily and Carly and their mom. "You've done so well hand-rearing them. They're so big and healthy-looking. You did an amazing job!"

Mom put her arm around Lily's

shoulders. "To be honest, it was mostly Lily. She's worked really hard—she even did some of the night feedings. I can't believe how big they are now. Seven weeks old! The time has gone by so fast."

Way too fast, Lily thought to herself.

"I guess if they were still with their mom, it would be too early for us to adopt them," Candace said thoughtfully. "It's very lucky for us, getting to have such small kittens. We're really grateful. Aren't we, Jack?"

Her little boy nodded. He had Bella on his lap, and he was running one finger carefully down her back all the way from the top of her head to her tail, over and over. Bella was nuzzling his hand, purring, and Jack looked as though his dream had come true.

Even though Lily hated the thought of someone else taking her beautiful kittens home, she could see that Candace and Jack were going to be amazing cat owners. *At least they're only taking Bella and Trixie*, she thought sadly. She wondered how Stanley would feel all on his own.

Stanley watched, confused, as the strange people put his sisters into a cat carrier. They were meowing, not sure what was happening, and he squeaked back anxiously. Where were they going?

And why wasn't he going, too?

He hurried to the edge of the plastic box as the kitchen door opened, and they all started to walk out—those people were taking his sisters away! Panicking, he clawed his way up the side of the box, his paws slipping, and scrambled out onto the floor to chase after them. But the door closed before he was halfway there, and he sat under the table and meowed frantically.

He jumped up when the door opened again and Lily let Hugo in. The big dog came nosing under the table and lowered his head to

Stanley. He licked the kitten with one great swipe of his huge pink tongue and then slumped down to the floor next to him, resting his muzzle between his paws.

Stanley patted at one of Hugo's long white paws, nibbled it, and then snuggled wearily into the kitten-sized space between Hugo's paw and his nose, curling up into a sad little ball.

Chapter Seven
Kitchen Chaos

"'Night, Mom." Lily peered around her mom's office door on her way to bed. "Oh, that one's so cute. Wow, you can really see how fluffy he's getting." Lily came into the room and leaned over her mom's shoulder, admiring the photographs of Stanley on her computer. "What are you looking at the pictures for? Are you sending them to

Grandma?" Lily's grandma loved cats, too. She lived in Canada, so she hadn't seen the kittens yet, but Lily had been telling her all about them on the phone. Grandma had told Lily how jealous she was.

Her mom looked up. "No, I wasn't. Maybe I should, though. I hadn't thought of that. I was actually looking for a good photograph to send to Amy for the rescue website. The one they've got up there now is all the kittens together—we need one of just Stanley on his own."

Lily took a step back, suddenly feeling breathless. Deep down, she knew that Stanley was going to be adopted, too. But this made it all too real—and too soon. He looked so cute

in the photograph on Mom's screen—
he had his mouth open in a meow, and
his little pink tongue was showing. His
eyes were shining emerald green, and
his fur was standing out around his head
in a fluffy halo. *Anybody would want to
adopt him,* Lily thought miserably. *Who
could resist such a handsome boy?*

"Oh, Lily...." Mom turned around in
her chair, reaching out to hug her. "I
know you love him...."

"Couldn't we keep him?" Lily pleaded. "He's so special…." Her voice wobbled, and her throat felt like it was closing up. She couldn't get any more words out.

"You know we were only taking care of them for a little while, sweetie."

Lily nodded and sniffed, then dashed out of Mom's office, racing upstairs to her bedroom. She flung herself down on her bed, burying her face in her pillow, her eyes full of tears. Why couldn't they keep Stanley? He got along so well with Hugo. Nora had been right when she said they made a perfect pair. Hugo had taken care of Stanley all morning after Bella and Trixie had left. In fact, Lily was sure that Hugo would be as upset as her if Stanley went to a new home.

She just had to explain all that to Mom and Dad. Lily rubbed her eyes and sniffed determinedly. Maybe she should write down a list of reasons to keep Stanley, just to make sure she didn't forget any of them. And then she would find just the right time to convince her family....

Lily woke up suddenly, her heart racing. She sat up in bed and peered around anxiously, trying to figure out what was wrong. Everything in her room looked strange and ghostly in the darkness. Why had she jumped awake like that?

She was just about to settle down

again, trying to smooth the crumpled
sheet and wishing the night wasn't
so hot, when loud barking erupted
downstairs—mixed with ear-splitting
yowls. Hugo was obviously furious;
it was his angry bark, over and
over again—and then there was a
crashing sound.

Lily flung back the sheet and headed
downstairs at a run, not even stopping
to think what was going on. Something
awful was happening. She could hear
voices in Mom and Dad's room—they'd
been woken up, too, and Carly appeared
in her bedroom doorway as Lily started
down the stairs.

She was surprised to see the kitchen
door was open, but then realized that
Mom and Dad must have left it ajar to

keep the room a little cooler so Hugo and Stanley could sleep. Hugo wouldn't come out of the kitchen anyway; he loved his basket. But maybe Stanley had come out of the kitchen and gotten lost in the dark. Had that crash been him knocking something over in the living room, maybe? That wouldn't make Hugo react so badly, though, would it? He was still barking—quieter barks now, and furious growls. Lily couldn't remember ever hearing him so upset.

Lily switched on the kitchen light, muttering, "Stanley? Hugo? What's the matter?" Then she gasped. The kitchen looked as though someone had run around pushing everything that he or she could find off the surfaces. The pile of newspapers from the recycling box was scattered all over the place. The vase of flowers that had been in the middle of the kitchen table was tipped over, cascading water down onto the tiles. There was even a mug smashed on the floor just below the sink.

Hugo was standing in front of the sink, growling angrily at the window above it. Lily shivered, suddenly wondering if there had been someone in the yard. Maybe Hugo had been woken by a burglar? Could he have made all this mess just by jumping around, trying to alert the family? Even though he wasn't usually clumsy, he did sometimes knock things over by flailing his tail around when he was really excited.

"It's okay, Hugo, shhh," Lily said. "What's wrong? And where's Stanley?" she added. When she'd gone to bed, Stanley had been curled up in Hugo's basket, snuggled in between Hugo's paws, and both of them had been asleep. There was no little white kitten in the dog basket now, or in the big plastic box.

"Stanley?" Lily called worriedly. Where was he? She ducked down, searching under the table and behind the garbage can, but there was no little white kitten.

"Lily, what's going on?" Dad hurried into the kitchen, with Mom and Carly close behind. "Wow! What happened here?"

"I don't know! Hugo's really upset, and I can't find Stanley. He isn't anywhere."

Hugo came over to Dad, sniffing and nosing at his hands, and Dad rubbed his ears comfortingly. "Hey, he's got a scratch on his nose," Dad said. "What happened, boy?"

"Oh, Hugo, did you cut yourself on that broken mug?" Mom crouched down to look, too.

Hugo pulled away and padded over to the sink cabinet again, this time leaping up and planting his paws on the edge of the sink. He wasn't supposed to jump up like that, but nobody stopped him.

Then a little white face peered out from behind the curtains. Stanley— with his long white fur all fluffed up. He was huddling in the corner of the windowsill, looking terrified.

"There he is!" Lily exclaimed gratefully. "How on earth did you get up there?" She hurried over to the windowsill, picking up Stanley and cuddling him close. She'd never have thought that Stanley could make the jump onto the counter—he must have jumped onto a chair to get him halfway. "Come on, Stanley, it's okay. What happened?"

"It's pretty obvious," Dad said anxiously. "They've been fighting. Hugo couldn't have cut his nose on that mug unless it actually fell on him. That's a cat scratch."

Lily could feel the white kitten's heart hammering, and his ears were laid back. Hugo dropped back down to the floor and stood looking up at Stanley in Lily's arms.

"That can't be right," Lily said, shaking her head. "Stanley loves Hugo.

They were even asleep together in Hugo's basket when I went to bed! And Hugo wouldn't hurt Stanley."

"He didn't!" Carly said angrily, crouching down beside Hugo and putting her arm around him. "Stanley hurt him! Look at his poor nose!"

Mom sighed. "We don't know which of them started it. I suppose we've been lucky we haven't had any issues with them until now—although it's weird that this happened so suddenly.... But if they're going to start fighting with each other, we'll have to talk to Amy in the morning. Stanley's old enough to stay at the rescue now until they find a home for him. Hopefully they've got room."

"What?" Lily gasped. "No, Mom — he's staying here. We said we'd take care of him until we found him a forever home. He can't go to the rescue!"

"He has to, Lily," Dad said gently. "I know you've loved having the kittens here, and you've worked so hard with them, but we can't risk Stanley getting hurt if he and Hugo aren't getting along. What if Stanley tries to scratch Hugo again and Hugo lashes out? I know Hugo wouldn't deliberately hurt him—at least I don't think he would—but he's just so much bigger than Stanley. It's not safe."

"And this is Hugo's home!" Carly put in.

"She's right, Lily," Dad said. "We can't send Hugo away."

Lily shook her head, tears starting to well up in her eyes. Stanley wriggled a little as one fell onto his nose and he licked it, liking the salty taste.

This can't be happening, Lily thought, looking miserably from Dad to Mom to Carly. Everyone seemed to be certain that Stanley had to go. *How did everything go so wrong?* Tomorrow was supposed to be the start of her grand plan to convince everyone that they could keep their beautiful kitten forever—and now instead, he was going to be sent to the rescue.

"He just can't," she whispered. "He'll hate it there. We saw the cats when we went to get Hugo—they had those little rooms. He's used to a big kitchen and my bedroom. He'll be so lonely without us." *And without Hugo*, Lily added in her head. She still couldn't understand what had happened. Hugo had never barked at the kittens—not even when he'd first found them in the woods. He'd taken care of them so carefully—Stanley even slept in his basket. This just didn't make sense.

But nobody was listening to her. It felt like all the plans were already made—Mom and Dad were discussing who could go and drop off Stanley at the rescue. Carly was still petting Hugo and glaring at the kitten.

"What are we going to do with them tonight?" Dad asked, looking between Stanley and Hugo. "We can't leave them both in here, obviously."

"I'll take Stanley upstairs with me," Lily said quickly. It was their last night, she realized. Her last time to cuddle him. "I'll take his box upstairs with me and put it by my bed."

Mom nodded. "Okay. But shut your door, Lily."

"I'll bring the box for you," Dad said. He picked it up and followed her up the stairs.

Lily couldn't help crying into Stanley's fur as she took him up to her room. He was still so little—much too little to go to the rescue, she was sure. It would be like sending him off for his first day of school. She half laughed, half sniffed at the thought.

"I'm going to miss this one," Dad said, rubbing one finger under Stanley's chin as Lily climbed into bed, still holding him. She put him down gently on top of the sheet, and Stanley started to wander around the folds, his paws sliding.

"Oh, Lily, don't cry, sweetheart." Dad put his arm around her. "He'll go to a wonderful new home. He's so handsome, he probably won't even be at the rescue for a day."

"I don't want him to have a new home," Lily sobbed. "I want him to stay here!"

"I know." Dad sighed. "I had been thinking about that, too…. But this is Hugo's home, Lily. You know that."

"I still can't believe they were fighting…," Lily whispered.

Stanley came stomping back up the bed toward her and began to climb onto her legs, wriggling as he got caught up in the sheet. Dad laughed and helped him up with a hand under his bottom. "There you go, Stanley.

111

'Night, Lily." He went over to close the bedroom window. "Just in case— we don't want Stanley getting out. I hope it's not too hot. Everything will be okay, honestly."

Lily watched him go, blowing her a kiss from the doorway and then closing the door behind him. *How can everything possibly be okay?* she thought sleepily as Stanley padded around and around on her tummy, making himself a comfy little nest. *It's not okay at all....*

Stanley tucked his nose under his tail and closed his eyes. He loved the feeling of snuggling on top of Lily. He could tell that there was something wrong — her breathing sounded different, with strange little hitches that made him bounce on her tummy each time. But he'd never been able to sleep on her bed before—it was even better than curling up next to Hugo. He was warm and safe....

His ears flattened back for a moment as he suddenly remembered, and he let out a little meow of fright. He'd been fast asleep, and then the barking had woken him. Stanley had never heard Hugo bark like that before—he was protecting his house. He'd been trying to protect Stanley, too, but the noise was still so scary.

Stanley had run wildly around the kitchen, trying to find a hiding place, but nowhere had felt safe. In the end he'd jumped onto the kitchen table and then made a flying leap onto the counter, scrambling frantically and almost falling back down. He'd huddled behind the curtains, curling up as small as he could as the barking and hissing went on and on.

Stanley stood up, pacing around and around on the bed to calm himself down. Lily shifted a little, with a wheezy moan, and settled again. Then, at last, they slept.

Chapter Eight
A Perfect Pair

"Do you think they'll want his toys at the rescue?" Mom said doubtfully, holding up a catnip mouse with half of its tail gone and a hole where the stuffing was coming out.

"He loves that mouse," Lily said, with a catch in her voice. "You have to take it!" She abandoned her cereal—she wasn't hungry, anyway—and got down on the kitchen floor, looking for all the jingly balls, feathers, and other toys that were scattered around. Of course, Stanley's favorite toy was Hugo, she realized, looking at both of them under the table. Mom and Dad had decided that as long as someone stayed with them the entire time, it was okay to let them be in the same room until Mom took Stanley to the rescue.

Hugo was lying stretched out under the table—probably hoping for Carly's toast crusts—and Stanley was playing with his paws. He was hopping over them, pouncing and patting at them with his own. Every so often Hugo would yawn and move a paw a little, so that Stanley leaped on it with ferocious tigerish growls.

Mom kept turning around from the bacon she was cooking and glancing over at them, obviously checking to make sure that they weren't about to fight again, but they weren't. It was a game; it always was. Lily stared at them, trying not to let herself start crying again. She still couldn't quite believe that this was happening. How could they be happy together now, when Hugo had been so furious last night and Stanley so terrified?

"Can you get that, Lily?" Mom said as the doorbell rang. "I don't want to leave this pan. It's probably just the mail carrier."

Lily got up and went to the door, opening it just as her dad came downstairs. Their next-door neighbor, Anna, was standing there, looking worried.

"Hi, Anna." Dad came over to the door. "Is everything all right?"

Anna smiled. "I hope so…. But I've come to apologize, just in case."

"Okay…," Dad said, looking puzzled. "Would you like some coffee? We're just having breakfast."

"Oh, I didn't mean to interrupt!"

"Honestly, it's fine."

"I'd love some coffee." Anna smiled and followed Lily and Dad through to the kitchen, where Mom was putting the bacon on the table.

"I do feel terrible, though," Anna continued. "I have a horrible feeling that Pixie's been in here again. She bolted in through the cat flap at about midnight. She was soaking wet, and all the fur that wasn't plastered down with water was sticking up. And I heard a lot of barking, so I wondered if she'd climbed through Lily's window again and had had a fight with Hugo….

You mentioned she'd come in that way before."

Anna looked between Mom and Dad as the entire family stared at her. "I really am sorry," she added. "I know she's a nightmare. My neighbors on the other side got very angry with her the other day—they found her on the kitchen table licking the butter…." Her voice trailed off. "Oh, no, what did she do?"

"It was Pixie!" Lily breathed, remembering her open bedroom window. "It was Pixie, not Stanley! Hugo was barking at Pixie!" And that meant Stanley didn't need to go….

"Mom, do you think…?" Lily put her hand on Mom's arm, trying to get her to listen, but Mom was looking at Anna and not paying attention.

"She was in here, then. Oh, dear...." Anna looked around the kitchen. "I really hope she didn't break anything."

Dad laughed. "Actually, I think she broke a mug, but don't worry, Anna. That's about the best news you could have given us. We came down last night because Hugo was barking his head off. We found the kitchen a total mess, and Hugo had a scratch on his nose. No, no, it's okay!" he added, seeing Anna put a hand up to her mouth. "You see, we thought it was Stanley who'd done it. We were going to take him to the animal rescue this morning, and now we don't have to!"

"Pixie scratched Hugo?" Anna looked down at Hugo guiltily. "Poor Hugo.

She's awful—she really is."

"But you love her," Mom said, laughing.

"I'd better start locking the cat flap at night." Anna sighed.

"Mom." Lily pulled at her sleeve. "Mom, listen, please—it's important. You need to call the rescue."

Mom gave her a hug. "It's okay, Lily. You don't need to tell me. We'll call them right now and let them know we don't need to bring Stanley in after all."

"I should have listened when you said that Hugo wouldn't have been barking like that at Stanley," Dad said, shaking his head. "I mean, just look at them."

Everyone looked down under the table. Stanley, worn out from his game, was collapsed over Hugo's enormous paws. As they stared at him, he opened one eye lazily, just a slit of green peering up at them all.

"Please…," Lily whispered. "Can we keep him? I know we had Hugo first, but Hugo loves him, too."

"Can we?" Carly put in. "It would make Hugo sad if he had to go," she admitted. "I think Stanley should stay."

"Yes! Oh, Carly, thank you!" Lily hugged her sister tightly.

Mom smiled. "I'd better go and call the rescue, shouldn't I?"

"What are you going to say to them?" Lily asked anxiously.

"I'm going to ask them to take his photograph off the website—he already has a home."

Lily threw her arms around her mom

and then her dad and even Anna—she wanted to hug everyone. Then she crouched down beside Stanley and Hugo. "You're staying," she said, petting the fluffy white fur on Stanley's tummy. "You're our kitten now!"

Stanley opened the other eye and stretched, rolling over onto his back and padding his front paws against Hugo's nose. Hugo snorted, shifted his head, and gently licked the little kitten.

Stanley uncurled himself from the

big dog and stood up, stretching again and arching his back as he yawned. He padded deliberately over to Lily and rubbed the side of his head lovingly up and down her shorts. He climbed onto her knees and stood up, nudging her chin with the top of his head and purring loudly. Then he jumped down and touched noses with Hugo.

"They're perfect," Lily whispered, crouching down to pet Hugo. "They belong together, here with us."

HOLLY WEBB

Holly Webb started out as a children's book editor, and wrote her first series for the publisher she worked for. She has been writing ever since, with more than 100 books to her name. Holly lives in England with her husband, three young sons, and several cats who are always nosing around when she is trying to type on her laptop.

For more information
about Holly Webb visit:

www.holly-webb.com
www.tigertalesbooks.com